PUPPY Club

LULU'S BIG SURPRISE

Catherine Jacob   Rachael Saunders

LITTLE TiGER

LONDON

KU-467-266

DUNDEE CITY
COUNCIL

CENTRAL CHILDREN'S

077 155X

ASKEWS £5·99

Puppy Club

Chapter 1

"We promise to love and protect puppies everywhere!"

Jaya, Willow, Harper and Elsa high-fived, as they did at the start of every Puppy Club meeting. It was Saturday afternoon and they were gathered in Jaya's playhouse, after spending the morning helping out at Underdogs, the rescue centre owned by her auntie Ashani.

Pictures of all kinds of dogs covered the walls and a large, handmade poster read:

Puppy Club Rules

1. Learn all we can about dog breeds.
2. Find out how to train puppies.
3. Share pictures of adorable puppies and dogs.
4. Show our parents what responsible dog owners we'd be.
5. If one of us gets a puppy, allow everyone to help look after it.

"You ready, Elsa?" Jaya asked, pulling her long dark hair off her face.

Elsa nodded eagerly. She smoothed down her paw-print-patterned skirt, opened up the club notebook on her lap, then paused. "Erm…" She wrinkled her freckled nose. "Can someone lend me a pen?"

"Here." Harper grinned, reaching into the top pocket of her dungarees. She pulled out a pen and handed it to Elsa. Harper loved to draw and never went anywhere without a spare pen and a sketchbook.

"Thanks," Elsa said, carefully writing the date in the club notebook.

"How come Elsa gets to take notes…" grumbled Willow, folding her arms across her red and white football shirt.

"She's Scribbler this month,

remember?" Jaya said patiently. "You're Picture Picker, Harper's Arts and Crafts and I'm Speaker, aka Top Dog. We'll swap again in a few weeks."

Willow rolled her dark eyes dramatically. "OK, fine," she huffed.

"So," Jaya continued, shifting on her beanbag to get comfy. "Today's meeting is about our class quiz. Ten questions on our favourite topic by Monday. Harper, our quiz is on puppy development. Elsa and Willow, you're doing puppy training. So—"

"Puppies!" Willow squealed, making everyone jump.

"Willow!" said Jaya, her hazel eyes flashing with impatience. "Talking here!"

"Sorry!" Willow giggled. "I just can't stop thinking about Lulu's puppies. They're going to be the most adorable balls of fluff EVER!"

Harper looked up from her sketchpad, where she'd been drawing a picture of Lulu. "It *is* the best news," she said, blowing her auburn fringe out of her green eyes.

"And she's having a scan tomorrow," Elsa added. "So we'll find out when they're due!"

Lulu was a new arrival at Underdogs. She had been handed in a fortnight ago, having been found wandering along the high street, and was named after a local bakery. Her fur had been matted and dirty but after a good wash they discovered she was actually cream and toffee-coloured, with a patch of chocolate. Nobody was quite sure what breed Lulu was but Jaya, who wanted to be a vet, had checked her dog books and reckoned she was a mix of poodle, spaniel and maybe terrier.

Lulu wasn't microchipped, so Ashani had put up posters and appealed online, but no one had come forward to claim her. After a few days at the centre, Ashani suspected Lulu was pregnant. Tomorrow's scan would confirm the details.

"I wonder what colour her pups will be?" Harper said dreamily.

"Well," Willow began, jumping up. "I think…"

Jaya glanced down at her puppy wristwatch and worked out they had only half an hour of the meeting left. "Come on, guys. I'm excited about the puppies too but we need to sort out our quizzes!"

"OK." Willow slumped down on her beanbag. Then she shot back up *again*. She was the tallest of them all, and her springy black curls almost brushed the playhouse ceiling as she hopped excitedly from foot to foot. "Hey, how *many* puppies do you think she'll have?"

Jaya threw her hands in the air. "I give up!"

"Sorry," Willow said, jumping around. "It's just too exciting."

"Six!" Harper cried.

Willow shook her head. "She's only little. I say four."

"Four's perfect." Elsa beamed, twirling a braid of pale blond hair round her finger. "One pup each!"

"If *only*," Harper wailed. "My parents say the same thing every time I ask – that they're far too busy and it wouldn't be fair to leave a puppy home alone all day."

"You've got more chance of your parents saying yes than I have," said Willow. "The only pet I'm allowed is a goldfish." She set her face into a frown. "No, Willow," she said in a voice that sounded just like her mum's. "We are *not*

getting a puppy. What about my nice new carpet? I don't want it covered in dog hair and muddy paw prints!"

They all laughed at Willow's perfect impression.

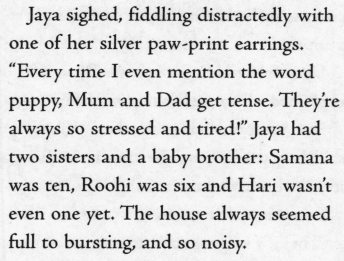

Jaya sighed, fiddling distractedly with one of her silver paw-print earrings. "Every time I even mention the word puppy, Mum and Dad get tense. They're always so stressed and tired!" Jaya had two sisters and a baby brother: Samana was ten, Roohi was six and Hari wasn't even one yet. The house always seemed full to bursting, and so noisy.

"I'd give anything for one of those puppies," said Elsa, a faraway look drifting into her pale blue eyes. "But Mum loves our cats too much. She's convinced cats and dogs don't mix."

"It's so unfair," Willow grumbled. "We'd

all be perfect puppy owners. We've learned loads helping out at Underdogs."

The four friends fell quiet.

"Hey!" Willow cried suddenly. "What if we work together ... to persuade our parents to let us each have one of Lulu's puppies?"

Jaya frowned. "Er, haven't we all just explained why none of them will let us?"

"But we could help each other," Willow said, her eyes shining. "To come up with ideas to bring them round?"

Elsa grinned. "Let's do it!"

"I'm in," Harper said. "How about you, Jaya?"

Jaya hesitated. She was pretty sure her parents would say no, whatever she did. Then again, she'd give anything for a puppy. It had to be worth a try. "OK. I guess so."

14

"Brilliant!" Willow reached out to high-five the others. "Let's call it … Operation Perfect Puppy!"

"Operation PAWfect Puppy, you mean!" Harper chipped in.

"Love it!" Willow beamed. "Operation PAWfect Puppy is GO!"

Chapter 2

After the excitement of Saturday, Sunday seemed to go on forever as Jaya waited for news of Lulu's scan. The morning had been busy with swim club and the usual family supermarket trip, but the afternoon was dragging. Jaya sat on her bed, dog books spread around her, as she checked through her puppy development quiz, but every question seemed to lead back to Lulu and her puppies. She'd got so sidetracked reading about how a vet can't always be certain a dog *is* actually pregnant, let alone how many puppies she's having, that she barely noticed the doorbell ring.

"Jaya," Mum called up. "Auntie Ashani's here."

Jaya threw the book she was reading on her bed and bounded downstairs.

Auntie Ashani was sitting in the

kitchen, with Hari gurgling away on her knee as Dad made faces at him.

"Hey, whirlwind. How're you?" asked Ashani.

Jaya hovered in front of her. "*I'm* fine! How's Lulu?"

"She's great. I have some news!"

Jaya held her breath.

"The vet confirmed she's pregnant and ..." Auntie Ashani hesitated, a smile spreading across her face, "she thinks there will be six pups."

"Six! That was Harper's guess!" Jaya cried. "But are you sure?"

Auntie Ashani nodded. "At least six. They're due in about three weeks. But the vet's worried Lulu might be feeling stressed at the rescue centre and has recommended peace and quiet until the puppies arrive."

"So where will she go?" asked Jaya, reaching for a chocolate biscuit from the open tin.

"She's moving in with me, this evening. I'm going to foster Lulu!"

"No way! We'll come and see her every day!" Jaya exclaimed. "We could even look after her while you're at Underdogs and—"

"Nice try," Mum interrupted. "But you're not skipping school."

Jaya frowned. "We can pop round though, can't we?"

Auntie Ashani smiled. "Of course, but the key thing is for Lulu to get some peace."

"Absolutely." Jaya's mind was whirring. "I can't WAIT to tell the others!"

"Honestly, Jaya," said Dad. "Do you four ever think about anything other than puppies?"

Jaya took a big bite of her chocolate biscuit. "Not often," she mumbled.

Dad laughed. "I didn't think so!"

"Imagine the cuteness, though." Jaya closed her eyes and smiled as she thought of six mini Lulus. Then she opened one eye and stole a glance at Mum. "I just hope they find better forever homes than Lulu did."

"Don't even think about it, Jaya," said Mum.

Jaya widened her eyes, trying to act all innocent. "About what?"

"About us getting a puppy."

"What? But Mum, I—"

"There's just no way. We've got our hands full as it is. Looking after you four is enough, without a puppy in tow."

Jaya looked pleadingly at Dad.

He turned to Hari and pulled another funny face. "What do you think, Hari? This place is so chaotic. Would we even notice a puppy?"

Mum glared at him. "Are you kidding?"

Dad held up his hands in surrender. "OK, you're probably right."

Suddenly Jaya didn't feel like finishing her biscuit.

Auntie Ashani reached over and

squeezed her hand. "How about you and the others visit Lulu at mine tomorrow after school?"

Jaya looked doubtfully at Mum. "Could you ask the other parents if that would be OK?"

Mum nodded.

"We can give Lulu a nice… Oh no!" Ashani jumped up as Hari sent his beaker of milk flying across the table.

Dad caught the beaker as Mum moved in with the kitchen roll. In the flurry, Jaya escaped into the garden. Mum's stern words rang in her ears and the joy she had felt about Lulu's scan and seeing her again dripped away like the spilled milk. Mum really didn't want a puppy. It seemed Operation Pawfect Puppy was over before it had even begun.

Jaya stomped through the overgrown

grass. She stopped to pick a feathery dandelion clock and held it up to her lips, screwing her eyes shut. "I wish I could have one of Lulu's puppies," she whispered. Then she opened her eyes, blew the dandelion seeds and watched as they drifted away on the breeze.

Chapter 3

"MUM! We're going to be late again!"
Jaya stood impatiently by the front door
amid the usual Monday morning chaos.

"I CAN'T FIND MY SHOE!" Roohi
hollered from the kitchen.

Moments later, Mum came steaming
down the hall, towing Roohi by the
hand.

Jaya rolled her eyes at her sister. "Don't

tell me, it was right where you left it?"

"*Actually* it was in Hari's toy box," Roohi said, sticking her tongue out and twisting one of her bunches round her finger.

"Stop bickering and let's go," said Mum, fastening Hari into his buggy.

Jaya sighed and opened the front door. Typical. They were going to be late on the one morning she'd wanted to be early so she could tell the others about Lulu.

They set off at a trot, Mum pushing Hari, and Jaya chivvying Roohi on. As they rounded the corner to school, Mrs Handy, the head teacher, was about to lock the gates.

"Morning, girls!" she said, beaming.

"Sorry we're late!" Jaya panted, hurrying past her and shooting an angry look at her sister.

In class, everyone already had their whiteboards out. Jaya slipped into her seat beside Harper and tried to focus. Usually she enjoyed mental maths but she was so impatient to share her news, she couldn't concentrate.

By break time, she was fit to burst. As soon as Mr Priest let them outside, Jaya dragged Willow, Elsa and Harper off to a corner of the playground to tell them.

"Oh my woofy word," Willow cried. "Six puppies!"

"Told you," Harper said, with a smile.

"At *least* six," said Jaya excitedly.

"So Lulu's staying with Ashani until she gives birth?" Elsa asked.

Jaya nodded. "And guess what, Auntie Ashani has invited us round to hers

26

after school today to see Lulu!"

"This is turning out to be the *best* day." Willow hugged herself. "And if Operation Pawfect Puppy works, they'll be *our* puppies soon!"

Jaya sighed, remembering her mum's stern words. "If only," she said. "Mum and Dad have practically said no to me already."

Harper elbowed her. "Come on, Jaya! Don't give up. We'll help you think of ways to convince them."

"Teamwork. Remember?" said Willow.

Elsa smiled. "This'll cheer you up. Mum says I can have a birthday sleepover, a week on Friday! My big brother's off to a friend's so we can watch the new *Puppy Spies* movie without him complaining it's babyish. Though I know secretly he's dying to see it!"

"Cool," Harper said.

Jaya felt better already. "I'm dying to see it too."

"And because it's my birthday on Wednesday," Elsa continued, "Mum says I can have you over for a birthday tea too."

"Group hug!" Willow cried and they all piled in.

The bell rang. Harper linked her arm through Jaya's. "Come on, Jaya. Quiz time!"

"Nobody's going to get all our questions right," Willow declared as they filed into class. "No one knows as much about puppies as we do!"

"Oh yeah?" A voice piped up behind them.

Jaya and the others spun round. Daniel and his best friend Arlo grinned at them. Daniel's bright green eyes twinkled with amusement behind his big, round glasses. He had sandy hair, which today was spiked up with gel. Arlo was a smidge taller, with closely cropped, tight black curls and mischievous dark eyes.

"Yeah!" said Willow.

Daniel smirked confidently. "We'll see…"

"C'mon," Arlo said, shoving him towards their desk.

Jaya caught Willow's eye and they both shook their heads. As if those boys would know as much about puppies as them.

Polly and Tess were first up with a football quiz. Sports fan Willow got every answer right. Next, Will and Jasmine did a planets quiz. Then it was Arlo and Daniel's turn. "So our quiz is about dogs." Daniel glanced over at Jaya and the others.

"What?" Jaya mouthed at Harper in surprise.

"We're going to give you three clues and you have to guess the breed," Arlo explained.

"Excellent!" said Mr Priest. "I love dogs. Off you go."

The boys' quiz was tricky even for Jaya. The last question was particularly tough: "Which breed originally came from Tibet, was a guard dog and has long shaggy fur?" Daniel asked.

Jaya wracked her brains then scribbled, *Lhasa Apso*. Sure enough, she was the only one to get ten out of ten.

"Well done, Jaya. Great quiz, boys!" said Mr Priest as Daniel and Arlo fist-bumped triumphantly.

Jaya and Harper were up next with their puppy development quiz. Both Arlo and Daniel got top marks *and* they scored ten out of ten for Willow and Elsa's puppy training quiz. Jaya couldn't believe it.

As the girls streamed out of class, Daniel called, "Those quizzes were tough!"

Jaya nodded. "So was yours."

"I didn't realize you two loved dogs so much," said Elsa.

Arlo nodded towards Daniel. "He's a walking dog encyclopedia."

"Oh yeah?" Willow shot back. "So's Jaya."

Arlo beamed. "And guess what? I'm getting my own dog. A puppy."

"Really?" Elsa cried.

"No way," said Willow.

32

"How did you persuade your parents?" Harper asked.

Arlo shrugged. "Dad thought it'd be nice for me and Sophie — that's my step-sister — to have a dog now we've all moved in together. We both love dogs."

"What breed are you going for?" Jaya asked.

"We haven't decided yet. We might look at rescue dogs."

"We know a rescue dog that's about to have puppies," Willow blurted out.

Arlo stopped in his tracks. "Really?"

Willow nodded. "Lulu. She's from the centre we help at."

"You help at a rescue centre? Awesome," said Daniel.

"My auntie owns it," Jaya added proudly. "Though we mainly just do back-room tasks."

"We go there every Saturday," Willow piped up again. "Before Puppy Club."

Elsa gasped and her cheeks flushed bright pink. Puppy Club was supposed to be a secret.

Willow clapped a hand over her mouth but it was too late.

"What's Puppy Club?" asked Daniel.

Harper jumped in. "Oh, you know, we just ... talk about puppies and stuff."

"Cool," said Daniel. "Can we join?"

"Erm…" Jaya hesitated. Elsa had turned away. Was she about to cry? She pulled Elsa towards the dinner hall. "C'mon. We'll miss lunch."

Harper and Willow scurried after them, leaving Arlo and Daniel looking confused. As soon as the boys were out of sight, Jaya rounded on Willow. "You told them about Puppy Club!"

"I know and I'm sorry," said Willow. "It just slipped out."

"The club's meant to be our special thing," Elsa snapped, her eyes glistening. "And now it's ruined."

Chapter 4

As the girls walked to Ashani's after school, the conversation quickly came round to Puppy Club and the boys. They'd had a row about it during lunch. Willow had stormed off to the toilets and Elsa had barely spoken since.

"Daniel asked again at home time about them joining," Harper whispered, trying to keep her voice down so Jaya's mum, who was walking ahead with Roohi and Hari, didn't overhear. "We'll have to give him an answer tomorrow."

"If only you'd kept quiet, Willow," Elsa hissed.

"I've told you twenty times, I didn't *mean* to," Willow snapped back. "And if you don't want them to join, we can just say so. Though *I* think they're fun *and* it's clear they love dogs."

"That's not the point," Elsa cried.

Jaya jumped in. "I like Daniel and Arlo too but I can see why Elsa's upset. Puppy Club is our special place."

"Actually, I kind of agree with Willow," said Harper. "And Arlo's even getting his own puppy. If they did join Puppy Club and helped out at Underdogs now and again, I'm sure

Ashani would be glad of the extra pairs of hands."

Elsa folded her arms. "Oh, so now they're coming to Underdogs too? Great."

"Let's talk about this later," said Jaya. "We're nearly at Ashani's and we're not supposed to stress Lulu out, remember?"

They walked the rest of the way in uncomfortable silence.

At Ashani's, Lulu was lying on a cushion

on the floor of the lounge, closely watched from the sofa by McFly, Ashani's big ginger cat.

"Hey, girl," Jaya said with a smile, crouching next to Lulu who rolled over for a tummy stroke.

Willow knelt beside her and ruffled Lulu's fluffy ears.

"She must be feeling tired," Harper whispered, softly stroking Lulu under her chin.

"Yes. She needs lots of rest," said Ashani. She glanced up at Elsa, who was standing by the door, her brow still crumpled in a frown.

"Aren't you going to say hello to Lulu, Elsa?" Ashani asked.

"I'll wait till Willow's finished," Elsa sniffed.

Ashani glanced at Willow, who didn't look up.

After they'd all had some time with Lulu, they followed Ashani into the kitchen.

"OK," she said. "Why the glum faces?"

To Jaya's surprise, Willow burst into tears. "Elsa's cross with me!"

Elsa looked shocked. "Willow, I…"

Ashani put one arm round Willow and the other round Elsa. "Why don't you tell me what happened? But first I think we're going to need some hot chocolate with squirty cream and marshmallows!"

With their steaming mugs in front of them, Ashani listened as the girls filled her in on their Puppy Club dilemma. "I can understand why you feel upset, Elsa," she said. "Puppy Club is so important to you all. But these two boys sound fun, and they're dog mad too."

"They are!" Willow sniffed.

"Daniel does know a lot about dogs," Elsa admitted.

"Well, how about you give them a trial?" Ashani suggested.

Jaya frowned. "What do you mean?"

"Perhaps Daniel and Arlo need to prove that they are worthy members of Puppy Club?" Ashani explained.

"But how?" asked Harper.

"Why don't they come along to Underdogs this Saturday? You do lots of jobs for me that aren't very exciting, but if they really love dogs they won't mind."

Jaya smiled. "And if they do well, we can all decide if we'd like them to join."

Ashani turned to Elsa. "What do you think?"

Elsa looked at her friends' hopeful faces and nodded slowly.

"How about you, Willow?" Ashani asked.

"Definitely." Willow reached for Elsa's hand. "I'm sorry."

Elsa smiled. "Me too."

The rest of the week flew by in a flurry of school stuff, Lulu updates and birthday sleepover excitement. Daniel and Arlo had readily agreed to the trial at Underdogs, and on Saturday morning the

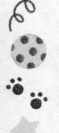

42

girls arrived to find them already waiting in Reception.

While the boys' dads filled in permission forms, Ashani explained what they'd be doing. "Now, you'll generally be in this area of the centre, where we do all the administration, food and medicine preparation. But don't worry, you'll get to meet some of the dogs too. We have one wing where we house dogs suitable for families with children, and you'll all get the chance to help groom and exercise one of those dogs. OK?"

Arlo and Daniel smiled and nodded.

As usual, it was non-stop. First task: wash and dry the breakfast bowls. Then they had to check the lunch timings list, fetch and prepare the next feeds and clean the grooming tools. Daniel and Arlo even threw themselves into the smelliest job of all…

"I don't mind doggy smells!" Arlo declared as they wheeled another barrow of poop towards the bins.

Even Elsa looked impressed. She hated that job!

After a short break came the best part of the morning. Sarita and Tom, both students who worked at Underdogs at the weekend, came looking for volunteers to help exercise Maggie, a gorgeous chocolate Labrador, and Bobo, a cute Yorkshire terrier who was moving in with a new family on Sunday. Jaya, Harper and Daniel volunteered to join Sarita playing fetch with Maggie out in the field.

Sarita was a veterinary student and a mine of useful animal information. "Why is it important to exercise older dogs?" she asked.

"Because it keeps their bones healthy and their weight down," replied Jaya.

Sarita nodded. "Exactly. And why is that particularly important for Labradors?"

"Because they're known for being a bit greedy and they sometimes overeat," Daniel called out.

"Top marks," said Sarita.

"Sounds a bit like my dad!" Harper laughed.

At the end of the morning, Ashani called them together. "You've all worked really hard. Did you enjoy yourselves?"

"We LOVED it!" cried Daniel.

Arlo nodded. "Best. Day. EVER!"

Ashani laughed. "Well, you're welcome any time."

Jaya stole a glance at Elsa, who was beaming and looked almost as impressed with the boys as Ashani.

But as Elsa opened her mouth to say something, the office door opened and Arlo's dad appeared.

"Hi!" said Ashani. "I was just telling the boys they've been stars today."

Arlo's dad looked pleased. "Sounds like you'll make a great dog owner, Arlo."

"You're getting a dog?" Ashani asked.

"We are. In fact, I wanted to talk to you about rescue dogs."

"You've come to the right place," Ashani joked. "One of our rescue dogs, Lulu, is expecting six puppies. She's staying at my house for now…"

While the grown-ups chatted in the office, the others waited outside. Jaya glanced at Willow and Harper, who were both looking at Elsa.

"So…" Elsa began, glancing at Arlo and Daniel. "What are you up to this afternoon? Only, we're having a Puppy Club meeting at Jaya's house … if you're free!"

"We are totally free," Daniel shot back.

"You bet," said Arlo. "So are you saying…"

Elsa looked at Jaya, Willow and Harper, who were nodding eagerly, then turned back to the boys and smiled. "Welcome to Puppy Club!" she said.

Chapter 5

Straight after lunch, Jaya headed out to the playhouse. There was barely room for four of them with all the garden toys, let alone six. She shifted out Roohi's old trike and the spacehopper and threw two sun-lounger cushions on the floor beside the beanbags. While she waited for everyone to arrive, she found a piece of cardboard and wrote: Lulu's Puppy

Countdown: 2 weeks to go! Then she wrote the days of the next two weeks down one side and PUPPIES DUE in big red letters next to the final Sunday.

As she was pinning the countdown chart to the wall, there was a knock. Arlo stood outside, holding a large, round tin. "Nice," he said, pointing at the wooden sign above the door:

Jaya smiled proudly. "Come in. It's going to be a bit of a squeeze."

Arlo stepped inside and gazed around. "This place is awesome. I love these pictures!"

"The sketches are Harper's," Jaya said. "And if any of us sees a great dog picture we print it out. I put this one up today." She pointed at a chocolate Labrador puppy running through long grass. "It reminded me of Maggie."

"Cool," said Arlo, plonking himself down on a beanbag.

The next moment the door flew open and Elsa, Harper and Willow piled in.

51

"What's in there?" asked Willow, pointing at Arlo's tin.

Arlo prised off the lid. "PAWsome cookies! I made them with my step-mum and Sophie last night."

"Pawfect!" Jaya giggled.

There was another knock. "Password?" Willow winked.

The girls grinned – they didn't actually have a password.

"Erm, woof?" Daniel called.

"Nope!" Willow laughed.

"Underdogs?" he tried.

"Uh-uh!"

"Erm ... puppy power?"

Everyone giggled.

"Come in," Willow shouted. "There isn't a password."

Daniel strode in, laughing. "Ha! Good one!"

"Hey, maybe we should make one up?" said Jaya.

"Puppies?" Willow suggested.

"Pawfect?" said Harper.

"How about ... Lulu!" Elsa cried.

"Yes!" said Jaya as everyone nodded. "Lulu it is. Now let's get started."

As they tucked into the cookies, the girls talked Daniel and Arlo through the club rules and the different roles.

"So we need to think of two new ones," said Jaya.

53

Daniel looked thoughtful. "Have you got a Fact Finder?"

"No, but that sounds right up your street," said Jaya as Elsa wrote it down in the club notebook.

Arlo swallowed a mouthful of cookie. "How about Snack Supremo?"

"Perfect," cried Willow, and everyone gave a thumbs up.

"Do you, like, have puppy code names and stuff?" asked Arlo.

"No," said Elsa. "But that's a great idea."

"How about we each choose the dog breed that suits our personality?" suggested Harper.

Willow jumped up so quickly she almost bumped her head on the ceiling. "Can I be Springer! Springer spaniel."

"Springer's spot on," Elsa said, laughing.

"Talking of spots," Harper added, "I'd like to be Dalmatian because of their gorgeous patterns."

"Labrador for me," Arlo said. "Clumsy but friendly."

Jaya thought that was perfect. "How about you, Elsa?"

"Well, I can be a bit shy until you get to know me, like my cousin's cockapoo."

"Cockapoo it is! That leaves me and Jaya," Daniel said.

"Well... I guess I can be a teensy bit bossy," Jaya began.

Willow gasped. "*Really?*"

Jaya laughed. "So I'll be Collie, as they're great at herding sheep!"

"And I'll be Greyhound," Daniel said. "I'm really fast."

Elsa wrote each of their code names in the notebook.

Jaya ... Collie
Elsa ... Cockapoo
Harper ... Dalmatian
Willow ... Springer
Arlo ... Labrador
Daniel... Greyhound

"So what do you normally do at club meetings?" asked Daniel.

"Well, whoever's Top Dog begins by asking if anyone has anything interesting to share," Jaya said.

"Usually we have loads," Elsa chipped in.

"But that was before Lulu," said Harper.

Jaya nodded. "Today's meeting is all about Lulu and putting Operation Pawfect Puppy into action."

"What's Operation Pawfect Puppy?" asked Arlo, puzzled.

The girls took it in turns to explain their plan to convince their parents to let them each have one of Lulu's puppies.

"So now you two have joined, we have six puppies and six club members," said Elsa.

"Do you want to be in on Operation Pawfect Puppy?" asked Jaya.

"You bet!" Arlo beamed.

"It's all right for you," moaned Daniel. "Your dad's already said yes."

"Not quite, but he did chat to Ashani

about Lulu's puppies earlier," said Arlo excitedly. "She said you guys are going to see Lulu tomorrow and we can come too!"

"That's Lulu, there." Willow pointed at a photograph on the wall of a little dog with big, floppy ears.

Arlo gazed at the picture. "What breed mix do you think she is?"

Daniel jumped in straight away. "I'd say she has some terrier in her, maybe a bit of miniature poodle and with those ears, spaniel too."

Jaya stared in amazement. That's exactly what she thought!

Arlo smiled. "Told you he's good."

"I *wish* Mum and Dad would let me have a dog," Daniel moaned.

"We all do," said Jaya.

"How exactly will Operation Pawfect Puppy work?" Arlo asked.

Elsa frowned. "Good question. Our parents all have different reasons for saying no. We have two cats, so I have to prove to Mum that dogs and cats can live happily together!"

"At least you have a puppy living next door, Elsa," Harper said.

Elsa's face lit up. "Pluto's a four-month-old Labradoodle," she told the boys.

"Hey, I read a story in the *Evening Post* about a dog that's been looking after a new kitten," Harper said. "I'll bring it to school tomorrow. You can show it to your mum!"

Elsa smiled at her friend. "Thanks, that would be great."

"My mum doesn't want muddy paw prints on her new carpet," moaned Willow. "On top of the mess my little

brothers make. They're so untidy."

"You'll just have to get on a cleaning mission, Willow," said Elsa.

Arlo nodded. "Elsa's right. Show your parents you can help keep the place tidy."

"Good idea," said Willow. "I don't mind hoovering actually ... well, it's better than washing up!"

"I've got some news," said Harper. "My dad's leaving his job and starting his own business."

Jaya looked thoughtful. "So he'll be working from home?"

Harper nodded. "*Exactly*. And when I pointed out a puppy wouldn't be on its own all day, he just smiled."

"Wow, Harper, you could be next!" Elsa exclaimed.

Jaya tried her best to look excited for Harper, but her mum's stern words swirled around her head.

"You OK, Jaya?" Elsa asked, noticing her friend's glum expression.

Jaya sighed. "I just don't think my parents will ever change their minds. They've already got more than enough on with me and my sisters, and a baby too."

Daniel frowned. "Do your sisters want a dog?"

Jaya shrugged. "I think so, but not as much as me."

"I bet they'd love a puppy! And maybe if you all worked together, you could persuade your parents? Teamwork, you know," said Daniel.

Jaya shook her head. "Teamwork?" Huh! Sam and Roohi would never agree."

"Well, it's worth a try," said Elsa.

  62

"My mum's always happy if me and my brother help with the chores."

Jaya thought for a moment. She could do more around the house, actually. They all could. "OK, but I still think I'm going to need a miracle to convince them," she said.

"You're not the only one," Daniel sighed. "I need to show my parents that my sister Violet's old enough to be trusted with a puppy, and I don't know if she even likes dogs."

"My brothers love playing puppies," said Willow. "I'm their owner and take them for walks and stuff. It's fun! It teaches them about puppy care too. Why don't you try that with Violet?"

Daniel smiled. "Thanks. I think she'd enjoy it!"

"See," Arlo said. "If we help each

other with Operation Pawfect Puppy we might all persuade our parents to get a puppy, right?"

Jaya crossed her fingers. "Let's hope so."

Chapter 6

Jaya lay in bed on Sunday morning, her head still buzzing with Operation Pawfect Puppy. She was just allowing herself to daydream about owning a puppy when the door burst open and Sam appeared. She was wearing her fluffy unicorn onesie and had tied her long dark hair up in a messy bun.

"Have you taken my hairbrush again?"

she asked, striding across the room and rifling through Jaya's desk.

Jaya sat up. "No!"

Sam picked up the latest copy of *Puppy Weekly* and smiled at the pug wearing a sparkly collar on the cover. "Wouldn't it be cool if we could have a puppy?" she said.

"SO cool," Jaya cried, then flung her head back on the pillow. "It's so unfair. Our own auntie's looking after a dog that's about to have puppies and Mum and Dad *still* won't say yes."

"Maybe they'll change their minds." Sam shrugged. "I'd help you look after it."

Jaya stared at her in surprise. "Would you?"

"Of course! You know I like dogs. Not as much as you and your puppy-obsessed friends, but it'd be pretty fun."

Jaya smiled. "Maybe you can tell Mum and Dad that?"

"OK," said Sam.

"Also, I was thinking…" Jaya began. "Maybe if we all helped a bit more around the house, Mum and Dad might be less stressed and keener on a puppy?"

"What? You mean do extra housework?"

Jaya thought for a moment. "If you help me with this … I promise I'll never go into your room without asking again!"

"Deal," said Sam. She sniffed the air. "Pancakes! Come on!" She bolted for the door.

Jaya pulled on her snuggly polar bear dressing gown and hurried after her.

"Shall we set the table, Mum?" Sam called as they ran into the kitchen.

Mum beamed. "Yes, please! That'd be great."

Jaya winked at Sam. Sometimes, her big sister wasn't so bad after all.

That afternoon, the Puppy Clubbers spent a few happy hours at Ashani's so the boys could get to know Lulu.

"Don't you want to keep a pup yourself, Ashani?" Arlo asked, fondling Lulu's ears.

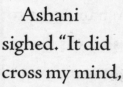

Ashani sighed. "It did cross my mind, but I'm afraid it's impossible when I'm at Underdogs all day, and sometimes all night too!"

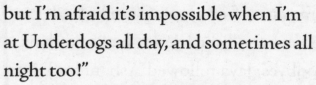

Daniel nodded. "Do you think the puppies will be the same colour as Lulu?"

"I honestly don't know," said Ashani. "She's such a mixture: cream, toffee, white, chocolate. The pups could be any or all of them."

"I can't WAIT to see them!" Willow cried.

Ashani smiled. "I know. But you won't be able to visit till they're around two weeks old. It's too stressful for the mother dog and we have to give Lulu and her babies time to bond."

The doorbell rang and Ashani went to answer it. A moment later she was back with Arlo's dad who was taking everyone home apart from Jaya. Once he had met Lulu and the friends had said their goodbyes, Jaya followed Ashani back into the lounge to wait for Mum.

"You've been very quiet this afternoon," said Ashani. "What's up?"

"It's the puppies," Jaya blurted out. "Arlo's parents are about to say yes. Harper's dad sounds keen too. But you heard Mum and Dad the other day…

70

What if I'm the only one who doesn't get a puppy?"

"For a start, that might not happen," said Ashani. "And even if it did, you'd still have five puppies to hang out with!"

Jaya sighed. "We have this thing – Operation Pawfect Puppy. We're helping each other try and convince our parents it's a good idea to get one of Lulu's pups!"

Ashani raised her eyebrows. "And how's it going?"

"Well, I'm trying to help out more around the house. Sam and I set the table this morning and I got Roohi to help me tidy the playroom before lunch. But I don't think it'll be enough to convince them." Jaya hesitated. "Would you speak to Mum for me, to see if you can change her mind?"

Ashani shook her head. "Sorry, Jaya.

It's not my place. You have to respect your parents' decision ... whatever it may be."

Jaya felt her cheeks flush. She immediately regretted that she'd asked.

Ashani pulled her in for a hug. "Shall I tell you a secret? When your mum was your age, the one thing in the world she wanted was ... a puppy!"

"What?" Jaya stared at her in shock.

"We both did. Desperately. Your mum pleaded with Granny for years, but she wouldn't budge. Grandpa was away with work for weeks on end so she was by herself a lot of the time. In the end, we gave up."

"Mum ... wanted a puppy?" Jaya said, unable to believe it.

Ashani smiled. "It might be worth reminding her how she felt back then. But if your parents really are against the idea, then I'm afraid you'll have to take no for an answer."

That night, Jaya's stomach churned as she lay in bed waiting for Mum to come and say goodnight.

After what seemed like forever, she poked her head round the door. "No dog books tonight?"

"No." Jaya eyed her nervously. "Mum, I've been thinking … about Lulu's puppies."

Mum rolled her eyes and sat down on the bed. "Yes?"

"Did *you* ever want a dog?"

Mum narrowed her eyes. "What has Auntie Ashani been saying?"

"Nothing!"

"Hmm. I'm not sure I believe you!" She sighed. "Yes, I did want a dog, more than anything else in the world."

Jaya smiled. "Just like me!"

"Just like you! But your granny and grandpa said it wasn't practical, and I'm sorry, Jaya, it's not practical now either."

"But Mum…"

There was a tap at the door and Dad came in. "Everything OK?"

"Yes. We're just having *another* puppy chat," Mum said wearily.

Dad sighed. "Jaya, Mum and I love dogs but…"

"Sam wants one too," Jaya blurted out. "She told me!"

Dad smiled. "And we'd get one tomorrow in a perfect world, but who'd feed and walk it while you're all at school?"

"A dog walker?" Jaya said hopefully.

"We can't afford that, Jaya," said Dad.

Mum shook her head. "And I'm run off my feet as it is without having to look after a dog every day." She kissed Jaya and flicked off the bedside light. "I'm sorry, darling. Lulu's gorgeous and I have no doubt her puppies will be too, but I don't think it would work. Now sleep!"

As Dad pulled the bedroom door to, Jaya was suddenly wide awake. Mum had said, "I don't *think* it would work…" That wasn't an outright no. And Dad had said they'd both love a dog too. Were they … softening a bit? Jaya snuggled under her duvet and shut her eyes tight. As she drifted off to sleep, her dreams were full of puppies.

Chapter 7

"Jaya! Over here!"

Jaya saw the Puppy Clubbers huddled by the playground bench, and she dashed over.

Willow pulled her into the circle. "Quick! Before the whistle. Arlo's got some news!"

Arlo beamed. "I'm getting one of Lulu's puppies. Dad confirmed it with Ashani yesterday!"

"That's brilliant," said Jaya, trying to ignore the sneaking niggle of jealousy.

"You're so lucky," Willow exclaimed, launching herself into a celebratory cartwheel.

"I know," Arlo continued breathlessly. "Sophie's super excited too."

Daniel high-fived Arlo. "Awesome! If my parents don't say yes, can I be your puppy helper?"

"Of course," Arlo said, laughing.

"One down, five to go for Operation

Pawfect Puppy," Harper cried. "The rest of us have to up our game."

Willow pulled open her rucksack. "That reminds me, Elsa. Here's that dog-and-kitten friendship article I mentioned."

"Amazing! Thanks, Willow," said Elsa. "I'll show Mum tonight."

"I tried extra hard to be helpful this morning," Jaya said. "That's why I'm actually here on time for once. I put the dishes in the dishwasher while Mum was in the shower, then helped Roohi find her reading book and fasten her shoes, so we were ready and waiting by the door. Mum couldn't believe her eyes!"

Willow smiled. "Great. I got a reward sticker last night for tidying up the twins' toys *and* I hoovered the hall carpet after they'd run inside with their wellies on. Mum pretended to faint with shock."

Jaya turned to Daniel. "How about you? Any joy?"

Daniel laughed. "I played Willow's puppy game with Violet when I got home on Saturday and yesterday she started woofing as soon as she woke up. We played it all morning and now she has so many questions... How much do puppies eat? How often do they sleep? She told us last night that she wants to be a dog when she grows up. Mum and Dad think it's hilarious. I'm exhausted!"

Everyone fell about laughing as Daniel gave a huge fake yawn and pretended to fall fast asleep.

"I got my dad chatting about his old sheepdog Dougal last night," Harper said. "He got out some family albums and showed me and Mum photos of them both when he was a kid."

"Fantastic!" Arlo said. "It will remind him how much fun he had with his dog."

"Ooh! I almost forgot," Elsa cried, turning to Arlo and Daniel. "Mum said your parents have agreed you can both come to my birthday tea on Wednesday too."

"Yes!" the boys chorused, fist-bumping one another.

Just then the whistle blew. Jaya linked arms with Elsa as they headed into school. "Double joy: birthday tea *and* your sleepover on Friday."

Elsa grinned. "I know. I can't believe I'm finally going to be nine!"

Wednesday whizzed around and as soon as school was over they all headed to Elsa's for her birthday tea.

"Happy Birthday, Cockapoo! Lots of

love, Springer!" Elsa smiled as she read out Willow's card. "Thanks, and I LOVE my puppy diary."

Harper handed Elsa her present. "I made the card myself."

Elsa opened it. Her pale blue eyes lit up. "It's a picture of me, Cockapoo!"

Harper had bought Elsa a book: *Teach Yourself to Draw Dogs.* Jaya gave her a photograph of Lulu in a dog-shaped frame and Arlo and Daniel had bought her a cuddly puppy they said was meant to look like a cockapoo.

Milo, Elsa's big brother, helped gather up the wrapping paper. "Now all you need is an *actual* puppy!"

Elsa sighed. "I wish."

"I can't promise that, but hopefully you'll like this..." Elsa's mum teased. She disappeared into the kitchen, and returned a minute later carrying a puppy-shaped cake, with chocolate-icing fur, jelly-bean eyes, strawberry-lace whiskers and chocolate-button ears. Nine candles fizzed on top. They sang "Happy Birthday" at the tops of their voices, but instead of "Elsa", they sang "Cockapoo".

Elsa bent down to blow out the candles.

"Make a wish!" said her mum.

Elsa screwed her eyes shut then blew them all out in one go.

Her mum winked at her. "I bet I can guess what you wished for. Is it furry and goes woof?"

As soon as they'd all devoured a slice of cake, everyone headed into the garden, where Elsa's two cats Juno and Lupo were enjoying the sunshine.

"How about a game of tig?" Willow suggested.

They were just deciding who would be "it" first, when there was a scrabbling sound from the hedge. Daniel ran over to investigate.

"Elsa! Look!" he cried out in amazement. "Your birthday wish has come true!"

Everyone turned to see a toffee-coloured

puppy wriggling under the hedge!

"It's Pluto! Next door's puppy," said
Elsa in alarm. "He's dug another hole!"

"He's adorable!" cooed Willow, bending
down to give the puppy a stroke.

Elsa ran over to catch him, but Juno
and Lupo had the same idea. They sprang
up, arched their backs and took off
after the puppy!

For a moment, it was mayhem, until Elsa finally managed to catch Pluto by his collar, just as Mum and Milo appeared.

Gently, Elsa's mum took the quivering puppy from her. "Here I was, worrying the cats would be scared of a puppy. Turns out it's the other way round!"

"I'm sorry, Pluto," said Elsa, giving him a reassuring stroke. "Those naughty cats!" The scared little Labradoodle nuzzled into Elsa's mum's arm. "You're OK, little fella," she said softly. "You're safe now."

Elsa was watching her mum with the biggest smile on her face.

Jaya smiled too. Elsa's mum looked as though she loved Pluto as much as Elsa!

When Arlo and Daniel's dads arrived to collect them, the conversation quickly turned to Lulu's puppies.

"I hear you're getting one of the rescue pups," said Daniel's dad as they waited for the boys to gather their things.

Arlo's dad nodded. "Well, after all the changes Arlo and Sophie have been through this year, what with the wedding and moving in together as a family, we think they've earned a puppy. What about you? Not tempted?"

"You know Daniel!" His dad smiled

over at him. "He's dog mad. He'd have one tomorrow."

"What about Violet?"

"Well, until recently we thought she was too young, but she's suddenly become puppy obsessed too!" he said. "Maybe a puppy isn't such a bad idea after all."

Daniel's mouth fell open. "Did you just say…?"

His dad held up his hands. "Now don't go getting your hopes up yet – there needs to be a *lot* of discussion before any decisions are made."

Arlo gave Daniel a celebratory whack on the back.

There was another knock at the door and Willow's mum came in with Willow's twin brothers Eli and Isaac. "Happy birthday, Elsa!" she cried. "Did

88

you get everything you wished for?"

Elsa glanced at her own mum. "More or less."

"Guess what," cried Willow. "Next door's puppy escaped into Elsa's garden and the cats chased him!"

Willow's mum rolled her eyes. "Seems I can't go anywhere without hearing the word puppy these days," she said as Jaya's dad and Harper's mum appeared behind her. "I'm seeing puppies in my sleep."

"Hopefully you'll see one when you're awake soon too," said Willow, laughing.

Willow's mum shook her head. "I've told you, Willow, we've just got new cream carpets…"

"If we get a cream-coloured puppy you wouldn't see the hairs," Willow fired back.

Everyone laughed.

"And didn't I hoover downstairs for

you yesterday and tidy away the boys' shoes?" Willow added.

Willow's mum smiled. "You did."

"I'm getting it from both sides in our house," Harper's mum chipped in. "Now Harper's dad's going to be working from home, he's started badgering me too. I'm outnumbered!"

Jaya waited for her own dad to join in the conversation, but he stayed quiet.

"See you girls on Friday for more birthday fun," Elsa's mum called as they headed off.

As they walked back to the car, Dad gave Jaya a quizzical look.

"You OK, Jaya?" he asked. "Did you have a good time?"

Jaya shrugged. "Yes. I had a lovely time. It's just ... do you think we'll *ever* get a puppy?"

90

Dad sighed. "You really don't give up, do you?"

Jaya hung her head sadly.

"Well," Dad said, putting his arm round her. "As my dad used to say, never say never!"

Chapter 8

Excitement prickled through Jaya as she wheeled her little blue suitcase towards Elsa's front door on Friday evening for the long-awaited birthday sleepover.

Elsa threw open the door. "Come on in! The others are already here!"

She towed Jaya into the kitchen where Harper and Willow were tucking into a plate of puppy-shaped cookies.

"Hi, Jaya," cried Harper. "I was just telling Willow that I've brought my face paints. Shall we all paint our faces as our Puppy Club code names?"

Jaya giggled. "Great idea, Dalmatian!"

So once they'd sampled the cookies, they took turns to transform each other into Collie, Dalmatian, Cockapoo and Spaniel. Of course, Willow got down on all fours and started woofing, sending them into fits of laughter.

The giggles continued as they arranged their pizza toppings into puppy faces.

"These black olives make great eyes," Jaya said, popping them on her pizza.

Willow looked at hers. "Mine needs whiskers. Ooh! I know!" She reached for a handful of green-pepper strips and arranged them around her cherry-tomato nose.

"Talking of puppies, is there any news about Lulu?" Elsa's mum asked.

"Yes," Jaya said. "I almost forgot. Ashani has moved Lulu into the whelping box."

"That's the cosy bedding area where

she will have her puppies," Elsa added.

"Not long to go then," said Elsa's mum.

"A week," the girls cried in unison and Jaya felt a fizz of nerves.

Once they'd eaten, they settled down to watch *Puppy Spies 2*. It was so good, even Willow managed to stay quiet during the whole thing.

"That was even better than the first movie!" Jaya said.

Elsa yawned. "I agree. That new pug character is so funny!"

"Time for bed, ladies," Elsa's mum called and they were all so full and sleepy, nobody argued. When she popped her head round the bedroom door ten minutes later they were already snuggled under the covers and before long, the whispered chat was replaced by the sound of Elsa snoring.

The next morning, Harper's dad arrived at nine to take them to Underdogs. Jaya smiled as she caught sight of her reflection in the car window, still with her puppy face paint on, though it looked a little smudged.

"Better be careful you aren't all mistaken for puppies!" Harper's dad chuckled. "Jaya, your collie make-up reminds me of my old dog Dougal."

Harper gave the others a wink.

"Did you know collies are the most intelligent dog breed?" Jaya said.

Harper's dad nodded. "Dougal was the cleverest sheep dog you'll ever meet. We got him at eight weeks old and he lived to the grand old age of fifteen."

"You were so lucky to have a puppy, Mr Ellis," Willow piped up.

"I know. Dougal was like my little brother in some ways."

Harper sighed loudly. "Oh, Dad, wouldn't it be lovely if we had a dog? It'd be like a little brother or sister for me!"

Harper's dad pulled into Underdogs, parked up and smiled at her. "You know

I'm on your side, Harper. Let me have another chat with Mum."

There was no time for being tired that morning. The boys met them in Reception and Suzy, Underdogs' assistant manager, explained that Ashani had stayed at home as Lulu had started to show some nesting behaviour.

Jaya's tummy did a nervous flip. "So Lulu might give birth soon?"

"It could still be a while yet," said Suzy. "Now, we have three dogs to get ready for their new families and I'd like you Puppy Clubbers to make sure they each have their favourite toy and blanket, then you can help give them a good groom."

They set to work. Along with Roger,

a young whippet, and an old bulldog called Rosie, it turned out Maggie was being rehomed too. As Jaya lovingly groomed Maggie's thick brown coat, she felt a pang of sadness.

"It's hard saying goodbye," Sarita said, noticing Jaya's downcast face.

Jaya nodded. "I'll miss her."

Sarita smiled. "I will too, but hey, Lulu's puppies will be here soon," she said, changing the subject. "Have you learned any new puppy facts recently?"

Jaya perked up. "I found out puppies are deaf when they're first born."

"Nice one!" said Sarita. "True of false: puppies are born without teeth?"

"True," Jaya shot back. "And they lose their baby teeth at three months. Ooh, and puppies don't open their eyes until at least ten days after they're born!"

Sarita gave her a thumbs up. "We'll make a vet of you yet."

After a hard morning's work, they found Harper's mum and dad waiting in Reception.

"Mum!" Harper cried. "What are *you* doing here?"

Harper's mum gave her a nervous smile. "Well, I wanted to be here when Dad told you the news…"

Harper's eyes widened. "News?"

Her dad beamed at her. "We're going to get one of Lulu's puppies!" he blurted out. "We phoned Ashani this morning and it's all sorted."

Harper's mouth dropped open. "Really?"

"Really!" Her dad laughed.

"How could I say no with you two giving me those puppy-dog eyes?" her mum joked.

"Thank you so much," Harper cried, tears of happiness trickling down her cheeks.

The Puppy Clubbers surrounded her, hugging and high-fiving. *Two down, four to go,* Jaya thought. If only she could be next.

After a quick lunch, Jaya sat in Puppy Club HQ waiting for the others to arrive. She was just crossing off the days on Lulu's chart when there was a rap on the door.

"Lulu!" A familiar voice called out.

Jaya giggled. "Come in, Dalmatian!"

Harper burst in, beaming.

"I'm so happy for you," said Jaya. "You must be pinching yourself!"

"I still can't believe it," Harper replied. "I hope it's you next, Jaya."

"Me too." But Jaya's stomach was in knots. Over lunch, she'd told her parents about Lulu's nesting behaviour but they'd seemed distracted with Hari. Jaya wasn't sure Mum had even noticed when she'd cleared the table without being

102

asked, though Dad had seemed pleased
when she and Sam had helped him put
the washing away earlier. He'd even
commented how well the sisters were
getting on. It felt good to be on the same
side for once, Jaya thought.

Elsa and Willow arrived together and
pulled Harper and Jaya into another
celebratory hug.

"You know, I think Dad's even more
excited than me," said Harper.

There was another knock. "Password?"
the girls cried.

"Lulu!" Arlo called, and he and Daniel
tumbled inside. Arlo had another
tin with him. Inside this time was an
enormous chocolate cake. "Well, I am
Snack Supremo," he said, grinning.

Daniel licked his lips. "It looks
awesome. Can we have a bit now?"

"Club business first," said Jaya impatiently. "Lulu could have her puppies any day and so far only two of us have managed to persuade our parents. Has anyone got any Operation Pawfect updates?"

Daniel's face lit up. "Violet's told Mum and Dad all she wants for her birthday is a puppy to love. Your dog game was a total winner, Willow. I think they might finally be coming round."

"Glad to help!" said Willow.

"My mum was in actual tears reading that article you gave me, Harper," Elsa reported. "The bit where the kitten is whimpering and the dog takes her to snuggle on her cushion. I even caught Milo reading it. And guess what? Mum has bought a little packet of dog treats, *just in case* Pluto gets into our garden

again and we need to tempt him back under the hedge."

"That's brilliant. It sounds as if your mum's softening too," Jaya said. "How about you, Springer, have you—" But before she could finish, there was a sharp knock at the door. "Password?" she called, frowning. Who could it be?

"Er, puppies?" came Mum's voice.

"No."

"Dogs?"

"Nope."

"OK, I give up," Mum called. "But I've got Ashani on the phone and she's very keen to speak to you all."

Jaya sprang up and yanked the door open. Mum stood outside grinning. She passed her mobile to Jaya. "You might want to put her on speaker, so you can all hear."

Jaya held the phone out to everyone. "Hi, Auntie Ashani," she said breathlessly. "Is everything OK?"

"Hello, Puppy Clubbers!" came Ashani's voice. "I have some news... Lulu has just had her puppies!"

Chapter 9

Once the excited squealing had stopped, they heard a ripple of laughter through the phone speaker. "It's a good job I haven't got you lot on loudspeaker here or you'd have frightened the puppies," said Ashani.

"But ... is everything OK? The puppies weren't due for another week," Jaya said anxiously.

"Remember, Lulu was already pregnant when she came to us, so it was never going to be exact," Ashani explained.

"I can't believe it," squealed Willow.

"The most important thing is that all six puppies are healthy," said Ashani. "There are three girls and three boys – they arrived about two hours ago."

Jaya's cheeks hurt, she was grinning so much.

"What colour are they?" Arlo called.

"A sort of dark toffee-ish colour, but that could change."

"How's Lulu?" Elsa asked.

"Exhausted but fine. I'll send a video to your mum shortly, Jaya, but I'd better get back to them now. Bye!"

"How wonderful," said Mum, taking the phone from Jaya. She looked almost as excited as Jaya felt. "I'll be back as

108

soon as the video arrives."

Once Mum had gone, pandemonium broke out again inside Puppy Club HQ.

"Three girls and three boys," Harper cried.

"Ooh, I'd love a girl," said Elsa dreamily.

"You can't have any at the moment," wailed Willow. "And neither can I!"

"Exactly," cried Jaya. "Look, it's brilliant news, but we need to get back to work on Operation Pawfect Puppy, or me, Greyhound, Springer and Cockapoo won't be getting a puppy at all." She bit her lip to stop herself from bursting into tears. It was all too much. "Springer, do you have an update?"

"Only that at lunchtime Mum was doubly cross because the twins had tipped out their craft box and left a glittery mess strewn over the carpet in the lounge, then Dad had been mowing the lawn and somehow managed to traipse grass all the way up the stair carpet too."

Daniel looked puzzled. "How's that related to Operation Pawfect Puppy?"

Willow explained. "Because guess who ran and tidied up the twins' mess and then grabbed the handheld vacuum and got rid of the grass?"

"You!" everyone chorused.

Willow beamed. "Mum said she couldn't believe how helpful I was being. She gave me two more reward stickers."

"Brilliant work, Willow," said Arlo.

"I'd happily hoover all day if it means Mum and Dad will say yes to a puppy," said Willow.

"Me too!" said Elsa.

Harper checked her watch. "It's been five minutes. Ashani *must* have sent the

110

video by now," she said impatiently.

"I'll go and check." Jaya sprinted up to the house. Mum was sitting at the kitchen table engrossed in her phone. As she looked up, Jaya saw tears in her eyes.

"Jaya!"

"Mum! What's wrong?"

"Wrong? Oh, nothing. But ... look!" She held up the phone. On the screen was Lulu, surrounded by six tiny puppies, their eyes screwed shut, nuzzling into her. "They're just ... so beautiful," Mum sniffed.

Jaya put her arm round Mum and stared in wonder at the puppies. "They really are, aren't they?"

Mum reached for her hand. Jaya clasped it and felt a sudden warm rush of hope.

The rest of the Puppy Club meeting was spent watching and rewatching the puppy video from Ashani.

"I want to snuggle them all," Willow said longingly.

"Me too," Elsa said and giggled.

"This is going to be the longest two weeks ever," moaned Daniel.

Arlo peered at the phone over Willow's shoulder. "I think I'm in love."

"Hey," Willow cried. "Could your mum forward the puppy video to our

parents? And any more that Ashani sends? I reckon once they see them they won't be able to resist!"

Jaya nodded. "Great idea. You should have seen Mum earlier. It was love at first sight."

At school on Monday, Daniel had promising news. "The puppy videos are working. Mum and Violet watched the latest one about twenty times last night. And Violet's named all the puppies!"

"My mum and dad loved them too," Jaya said, thinking back to the previous night when the whole family had crowded round after tea to watch them. "But I still don't think it's enough to convince them. I got up extra early again this morning to help with breakfast, fill the water bottles, pack Roohi's bag and fasten her shoes while Mum got Hari in the buggy. She said she must be dreaming! I just hope I've done enough to show her a puppy wouldn't be too much extra effort, especially if we're all helping out."

On Wednesday, for Daniel anyway, there was good news: his parents had said yes!

The pressure was really on now for Jaya, Elsa and Willow.

Ashani sent daily puppy-video updates, which Jaya's mum shared on the Puppy Club parents' group chat. They all pored over them at home every evening, then at school they discussed

which puppy had changed colour, which would be the first to open its eyes, which seemed the cheekiest…

By the time Saturday came round, the Puppy Clubbers were desperate to pounce on Ashani at Underdogs, so when she popped in for half an hour she was met with a barrage of questions. How were the puppies sleeping? Were they all feeding OK? Was all the puppy poop very smelly?

"Slow down!" Ashani laughed. "They're actually sleeping very well. It's pretty much their main activity. Lulu's a great mum and she makes sure they all get their fair share of milk, even the quieter, less pushy pups. And yes, it is a little smelly, but it won't be forever." She took out her mobile phone. "Here's a video of them exercising this morning."

They gathered round and watched
Lulu and the pups exploring Ashani's
back garden. Most of them stuck fairly
close to Lulu, except for one, who kept
running off towards the fence.

"That one's adventurous," said Willow.

"Yes. I call him Wriggler. He's always
on the move." Ashani smiled and put
her phone away. "Now I have a question

116

for Jaya, Elsa and Willow. How are you getting on with Operation Pawfect Puppy – any luck?"

They all shook their heads.

"Only, word has spread about the puppies through our social media pages and we've had a number of enquiries. I know how hard this is but I can't put them off forever. I think it's time to ask your parents for a decision."

"But what if they say no?" Jaya cried.

"Then I'm afraid you three will have to respect their decision. Look, how about we have a meeting with everyone – you six, and all your parents?"

Willow frowned. "Like a Puppy Club meeting, but with grown-ups?"

Ashani nodded. "Exactly. We can hold it here at Underdogs. Arlo, Daniel and Harper's parents have already sent me lots of queries. This way, everyone can ask me any questions they might have, and the remaining parents can make their final decision."

Final. Jaya's stomach churned.

"I'll fix a date for next week — maybe Wednesday?" Ashani paused. "I know it's hard, but if your parents don't say yes, I'll need to look at finding excellent homes for the three remaining puppies. OK?"

Jaya nodded. This was it. Soon she would know for sure, one way or another.

Chapter 10

By the time Wednesday's meeting rolled around, Jaya was a bag of nerves. Despite everyone's best efforts, they'd had no further Operation Pawfect Puppy successes.

She looked round the Underdogs' office. It felt strange being there with their parents.

"Good evening," Ashani began. "And

thank you to Jaya, Harper, Willow, Elsa, Daniel and Arlo, for accepting us grown-ups into this extraordinary meeting of Puppy Club ... for one night only!"

Everyone laughed, even Mum, which made Jaya feel a teensy bit better.

"So my job is to find Lulu's remaining three puppies forever homes," said Ashani. "Some of you have already agreed to take a puppy. For those still considering, there is absolutely no pressure at all. We've had lots of enquiries so the pups will end up with loving homes, whatever you decide."

Jaya stole a glance at her mum and dad but they weren't giving anything away.

"The puppies will be ready to go to their forever homes in just under seven weeks," Ashani continued. "They'll be fully health-checked and microchipped and will have had their first set of injections. So I must begin by telling you that puppies are like babies ... hard work!"

Nervous laughter rippled around the room.

"Hmph!" Mum muttered, making Jaya squirm.

"Will we be back to sleepless nights then?" Daniel's dad asked.

Ashani laughed. "Depends on the puppy. I've always used a crate at night. Some owners sleep next to their new pup to comfort them."

"You must be kidding!" Jaya's dad exclaimed.

Jaya thought she wouldn't mind that a bit. She'd sleep *in* the crate if it helped her puppy to feel loved.

"Is it true they sleep for eighteen hours a day at first?" Elsa's mum asked.

Ashani nodded. "Puppies need loads of sleep to grow, and of course, they need to be toilet trained too."

"Ugh!" said Willow's mum, screwing up her nose.

Willow gave a funny little gasp and Jaya was surprised to see her friend's

eyes brimming with tears.

"You OK?" Willow's mum mouthed.

Willow pursed her lips and nodded firmly, determined not to cry, but she was clearly very upset.

Her mum reached over and gave Willow's hand a squeeze. "Do you know if Lulu's puppies will shed fur?" she asked Ashani in a brighter voice.

"All puppies tend to shed a bit of hair at first," said Ashani.

Willow shot her mum and dad a wobbly smile. "But remember how good I've been with the vacuuming." She gazed up at them eagerly.

Her parents smiled at each other.

"True. And fur aside, I can't imagine a puppy could ever be as messy as your brothers," said her mum.

Willow's eyes widened. "Exactly. So

123

can we…?" she whispered.

Willow's dad raised one eyebrow at her mum, who gave a tiny nod.

"If it's a yes from Mum … it's a yes from me," her dad said, beaming.

Willow's mouth dropped open. "What? Really?" she shrieked.

"As long as you continue to keep on top of the hoovering!" her mum warned.

Willow bear-hugged them both, then jumped up and ran round high-fiving Jaya and the others.

"No pressure on us now then," Jaya's mum muttered.

Ashani waited for Willow to sit down before speaking again. "Now I'd also suggest signing up for a puppy-training class. Socializing with other dogs is important. And of course you need to be aware that puppies love to chew.

So keep any precious objects out of reach. Cost-wise, there's food and vet's bills and all the puppy paraphernalia to consider too..." Ashani paused and smiled. "There's no getting round it, puppies are a big commitment. But they're super rewarding too. So are there any questions?"

"I've been worrying about our two cats," said Elsa's mum. "But I've been reading lots and it sounds as though they might get on better than I thought..."

Ashani nodded. "It can take a bit of time, but after a shaky start my cat and Lulu get on pretty well. He doesn't even mind her puppies!"

"Told you," Elsa cried, tugging on her mum's arm. "*Please*, Mum."

Her mum sighed. "It's a strong maybe, Elsa. But I need to sleep on it."

Jaya looked pleadingly at her mum and dad. Dad gave her hand a comforting squeeze but Mum stared straight ahead.

Ashani glanced around the room. "Well, if nobody else has any more questions, we'll leave it there. So we now have four confirmed puppy owners. If anyone changes their mind over the next few days that's absolutely fine, but it'd be a great help to know everyone's final decision by the weekend."

That evening, as Jaya was watching TV with Sam and her parents, Mum's phone beeped. "It's Elsa, for you on the parents' group chat," said Mum, scrolling through the message.

Jaya listened nervously as Mum read it out.

Mum's said yes! I'm getting a puppy!

Jaya forced a smile, though she felt like crying. "That's … brilliant!"

Sam jumped off the sofa and glared at her parents. "Come on, guys! Jaya's the only one left now! You can't keep holding out when every single one of her friends' parents have said yes."

Dad peered sternly at Sam. "While it's great you have your sister's back, Samana, this is not your decision."

"Sorry," Sam huffed. "It's just … well, I'd actually like a dog too. I've told you I'd help Jaya look after it."

Jaya could have hugged her! She waited for Mum or Dad to say something, but neither of them did. Sam shook her head and shot Jaya a despairing look.

Jaya bit her lip to stop herself from crying. "Can I type a message back to Elsa, Mum?" she asked.

"Of course." Mum handed her the phone. Jaya typed:

So happy for you!

But as she added a line of puppy emojis, one of the tears that had been wobbling on her eyelashes escaped and rolled down her cheek. She brushed it away as she handed

Mum the phone. Jaya's worst fear had come true: she was the only member of Puppy Club who wouldn't have a puppy after all.

The next morning, Jaya was last down to the kitchen for breakfast. She didn't feel like eating.

"Morning," she muttered.

"Morning!" Sam sang back, sounding much more cheerful than last night.

Dad held his hand up for a high five, which Jaya half-heartedly returned.

"Beautiful morning!" Dad said.

"Is it?" Jaya sniffed.

Mum hummed a tune while she poured Jaya some orange juice. Jaya stared at her. How could they be so happy when they knew she felt so miserable?

Mum sat down next to her. "Jaya, we

know how upset you are, with all your friends getting a puppy, but…"

"I know," Jaya said flatly. "It's not the right time. Too expensive. You don't need to tell me again."

"Well, actually…" Dad began, glancing at Mum. "Mum and I had a chat last night."

"And me," Sam said.

Dad smiled at Sam. "Yes, Sam too…"

Jaya's heart began to beat a little faster. "What … kind of chat?"

"Well…" Mum paused. "We know how much this puppy means to you and how hard you've been trying to help around the house and get on with your sisters. Dad and I have been really impressed…"

Jaya stared at Mum. Then at Dad. They were both beaming. Sam too. "We're not, are we?" Jaya whispered.

"Are we getting the final puppy?"

Mum's smile stretched even wider.
"We are."

Sam and Roohi started squealing and
whooping and Hari banged his spoon.
Jaya sprang up and drew her parents into
a hug. Her legs suddenly felt wobbly.
"Thank you SO MUCH!"

"We chatted to Ashani last night and she'll help us out on the evenings you girls are really busy," Mum explained, escaping Jaya's squeeze. "And Sam and Roohi will muck in too," Mum continued.

"Course we will," Sam cried.

"Can I be in charge of grooming?" Roohi asked excitedly.

"Ask Jaya," Mum said. "Ultimately, this is her puppy and her responsibility."

Happy tears were now flowing down Jaya's face. "Somebody pinch me!"

Dad laughed and pinched her lightly on the arm.

"I won't let you down," Jaya cried. "I'll be the best puppy owner ever!"

Chapter 11

Jaya dashed into the playground and made a beeline for her friends, who were huddled around the bench.

"Jaya! I'm so sorry that you're the only one left," said Elsa, jumping up and giving her a hug.

"It's *so* not fair," said Willow. "Operation Pawfect Puppy was meant to be for all of us and now—"

"Guys! Breaking news!" Jaya interrupted, grinning round at their surprised faces. "Mum and Dad said *yes!*"

Everyone stared, open-mouthed.

Arlo was the first to recover. "You're getting the last puppy!" he yelled.

"I am!" Jaya laughed as they all flew towards her for a group hug. "We did it. Operation Pawfect Puppy has been a success!"

Over the next two days, the Puppy Clubbers' excitement levels shot up even further with every minute that ticked towards meeting their puppies. Finally, on Saturday morning, exactly two weeks after the puppies were born, it was time for their first visit.

Instead of going to Underdogs, they

headed straight to Ashani's, where they'd agreed to go in one at a time so they didn't stress Lulu out.

When it came to Jaya's turn, she didn't think she'd ever felt so excited in her whole life. Her tummy was fluttering with a million butterflies and her hand shook as she pushed the lounge door open and crept in. But then her gaze fell on the whelping box and all the nerves flew away.

The six puppies were nestled around Lulu. They were even more beautiful than she'd imagined. Jaya stepped a little closer. Five puppies had their eyes open. One's remained closed. Four of them were a lighter beige colour, one was darker brown and the one with its eyes shut was almost white. Jaya giggled quietly as one of the beige pups wriggled around.

135

"That's the one I call Wriggler,"
Ashani whispered behind her. "He never
stays still!"

Jaya watched as Lulu licked and nosed
the pup. "I just can't believe one of you
is mine," she whispered.

Once they'd all been in to meet the
puppies, they gathered around the table
in the kitchen.

"They're the most gorgeous things
ever!" Willow exclaimed.

"Adorable!" Elsa cried.

"Which was your favourite?" Arlo
asked.

"I couldn't choose," Harper said.

"Me neither," Daniel replied, smiling.

Jaya just nodded dreamily, images of
the beautiful puppies filling her head.

One by one, their parents popped over to collect them until only Jaya was left. Finally, Mum arrived with Roohi, Sam and Hari and they all tiptoed in to meet the puppies. As his big sisters cooed over them, Hari pointed and gurgled from Ashani's arms.

Mum smiled. "Hey, do you remember what we'd planned to call our puppies, Ashani, *if* Mum had ever agreed?" she asked in a hushed voice.

Ashani nodded. "Razzle and Dazzle!"

Mum gazed into the whelping box. "Look at them, snuggled up with their mum." Her smile faded. "Poor Lulu, having to go back to the rescue centre."

"Well…" Ashani hesitated. "Do you want to know a secret?"

"Yes!" everyone whispered.

"OK, the staff don't know yet but … Lulu *isn't* going back to Underdogs. I've become so attached to her these last few weeks I can't bear to part with her. So ... I'm going to adopt her!"

Mum sprang up and gave her sister a long hug.

Jaya gasped. "So our puppies will still get to see their mum. That's the best news ever!"

A few weeks later...

Jaya, Harper, Elsa, Willow, Arlo and Daniel had gathered at Ashani's house. The puppies were five weeks old and growing fast. The Puppy Clubbers had been to visit them every week and, best of all, they were now allowed to hold them, though it would be another three weeks before they could take them home.

Jaya sat with her friends on the floor, cradling a calm, sleepy puppy. Today was a big day: time to officially choose their puppies! Of course, they already knew which each of them would choose. They'd all had clear favourites almost from the start and puppy names had been a huge topic of conversation!

First up, Arlo, who'd fallen for the white and toffee-coloured male that Ashani had nicknamed Wriggler. "He's wriggly *and* fast," said Arlo. "So I'm calling him Dash!"

Ashani grinned. "Goodbye, Wriggler. Hello, Dash!"

Next, Harper smiled down at the white puppy with two black-tipped ears who was snoozing in her lap. "Meet Minnie. She has black ears just like Minnie Mouse."

  142

Daniel's choice was the greediest pup, who was always first to the food. He was fluffy and golden like a teddy bear, so the name Teddy seemed perfect.

Next, Willow held up her cream ball of fluff and waved his left paw, to show a toffee-coloured patch of fur in the shape of a large peanut. "Say hello, Peanut," she said, giggling.

Elsa smiled at the chocolate, tufty pup in her lap, who for once was sitting quietly instead of yapping at her brothers and sisters. "This is Coco — she's a feisty little thing, and she'll need to be, to deal with Juno and Lupo!"

Jaya gazed lovingly at the pale ball of fur, fast asleep on her own knee. "And this," she whispered, "is Bonnie. Because she is just that."

They spent the next hour trying to

get the puppies used to their names and making lists of supplies they were going to need. After all, with only three weeks to go before the puppies came home, they had a *lot* of preparation to do.

Operation Pawfect Puppy was far from over. In fact, it was only just beginning.

Think you know your Dalmatians from your Labradors? Test your knowledge with **Daniel and Arlo's dog breed quiz!**

1. Which breed is a great swimmer, a cross between a poodle and a Labrador and can be either really big or really small?

2. Which German breed is named after a place in France? It was used for herding and guarding sheep and often works for the police and the army?

3. Which breed is intelligent, has a great sense of smell and a soft mouth?

4. Which breed originated in Germany, is an expert at fitting into small tunnels and is also known as a sausage dog?

5. Which breed loves people, has two different types (working and show), and starred in *The Lady and the Tramp*?

6. Which breed is named after a place in Croatia, is covered in spots and makes you think of the number 101?

7. Which breed is the smallest in the world, originated in Mexico and can run very fast?

8. Which breed is originally from the

Swiss Alps, is often seen with a barrel of brandy round its neck and is known for mountain rescues?

9. Which breed comes from Ireland, has reddish fur and a long silky coat?

10. Which breed originally came from Tibet, was bred to be a guard dog and has long shaggy fur?

Answers: 1. Labradoodle 2. Alsatian/German Shepherd
3. Golden Retriever 4. Dachshund 5. Cocker Spaniel
6. Dalmatian 7. Chihuahua 8. Saint Bernard 9. Red Setter
10. Lhasa Apso

Feeling peckish?
Try Arlo's PAWfect cookie recipe

You will need a grown-up to help
you with this recipe.
This will make about 15–20 cookies.
Pre-heat the oven to 190 degrees C
or gas mark 5.

Ingredients

For the biscuits:
250g plain flour (or gluten-free if
preferred)
125g butter
125g brown sugar
1 small egg, beaten
(Paw-shaped cookie cutter optional!)

For the icing:
125g icing sugar
1-2 tablespoons hot water (ask your
grown-up for help with this)
writing icing pen for the paw print design

Method:

Mix the butter and sugar together in a
bowl until fluffy. Beat in the egg a little
at a time.

Sift in the flour and mix well till it forms
a ball of firm dough.

 Roll out the dough until it is about the
thickness of a £1 coin. Cut out the paw-
shaped biscuits using the cutter, or
free-hand, then transfer to baking sheets.

Ask your grown-up to help you put the baking sheets in the oven. Bake for around 10 minutes until light brown. With help from your grown-up remove the biscuits from the oven and leave to cool.

For the icing:
With help from your grown-up mix the icing sugar and hot water together in a bowl until smooth.

Spoon the icing on to each one and spread. Leave to set. Then using the icing writing pen, decorate your biscuits with a paw-print design.

Enjoy your pawfect cookies!

Can't wait for the next book?
Turn the page
for a sneaky peek…

Chapter 1

"HISS!"

"WOOF!"

"MIAOOOOW!"

"Someone catch Coco!" Elsa yelled
above the din, as her tiny puppy tore
round the sofa with two huge cats hot on
her chocolate-brown tail.

The six Puppy Clubbers were
gathered at Elsa's for their weekly

meeting, but calm had turned to chaos after Elsa's brother Milo left the sitting-room door open. Then, the family cats Juno and Lupo had darted in, cornered Coco in a pincer movement, and pounced! Luckily, Coco had leaped out of the way, but now everyone was trying to rescue the terrified puppy as she skittered across the wooden floor.

"Grab the cats!" Elsa shouted at Milo.

"I'm trying!" he shot back, finally making a successful grab for Juno.

Then Mum appeared, grim-faced. "What on earth is going on?"

Coco sidled over to Elsa, whimpering. Elsa plucked the tiny puppy up into her arms and cuddled her tight. "It's the cats' fault," she said crossly.

Mum bent down and picked up Lupo, who now there was no puppy to chase, had stopped to wash her tail.

"Elsa, didn't we agree to keep Coco and the cats apart until they start to get along?" Mum said. "Coco's your responsibility!"

"But—" began Elsa.

Mum held up her hand. "No buts. She's your puppy." She took Lupo into the kitchen and returned for Juno, who was struggling in Milo's arms, before shutting the door behind her.

There was an awkward silence. Elsa blinked away angry tears. She hated being told off in front of her friends. She glared at Milo. "That was your fault! You *know* you're supposed to shut the kitchen door so the cats can't get to Coco!"

Milo snatched up his comic. "I'm sorry, OK!" he said, storming out the room.

"Oh my gosh, Elsa! Poor you! And

poor Coco," Jaya cried, reaching over to stroke Coco's ears.

Arlo held out the tin of cookies he brought. "Make you feel better?"

Elsa shook her head.

"Those cats are fast," said Daniel.

Willow nodded. "They've really got it in for Coco."

Elsa groaned. This was not making her feel any better.

Harper put her arm round Elsa. "I'm sure they'll get used to her ... eventually."

"Will they?" said Elsa, slumping on to the sofa with Coco on her knee.

"I'm sure they will," said Arlo. "Look, everything's OK now."

"Everything's *not* OK!" Elsa said, her voice breaking with emotion. "Ever since Coco arrived, the cats have been awful! She just wants to be friends but they always hiss at her or swipe a paw, or chase her! That's why we're trying to keep them apart. But it's not working. Mum's so stressed and I'm worried…" Elsa paused, not wanting to voice her worst fear.

"What?" Daniel asked, looking puzzled.

"That she'll send Coco back to Underdogs!" Elsa blurted out.

Catherine Jacob loves writing stories for children and also loves dogs, so *Puppy Club* is a dream to write. She lives in Yorkshire with her husband, three young children and a Labradoodle puppy. Many of the *Puppy Club* puppies' escapades are based on real life events!

Catherine is also passionate about the environment and as a TV reporter, she has travelled around the world, including the Arctic and the Amazon, but she's happiest back at her writing desk, drinking tea and eating biscuits.

Hailing from Hampshire, Rachael Saunders
is an illustrator with a passion for storytelling
and character design. Her distinctive, bright
and joyful work spans the worlds of children's
literature, animation, product design
and handbags.

When she's not creating beautifully whimsical
illustrations, she can be found playing tennis
or getting lost in the New Forest while
walking her dog.